King of the Castle

Neil halted and slapped his leg to bring Sam back to his side as first King, then Penny, appeared round a turn in the path. Penny also halted abruptly and said, "Oh, it's you again."

Neil thought she was giving him the sort of look she would give to a slug in her salad. The Great Dane stood beside her, head up, on guard, until Penny said, "All right, King." Then he paced across the clearing, nosed Neil in a friendly way and dipped his head to sniff at Sam. Sam, who was used to meeting lots of strange dogs at King Street, gave him a friendly sniff in return.

Neil took out a dog treat, and while King ate it he had another look at his eyes. They were watering again, and some of the fluid had dried and crusted around King's eyelids. The eyes themselves looked inflamed. Neil suddenly felt furious. Couldn't the Ainsworths see what was wrong with this great dog? Didn't they care?

More Puppy Patrol stories follow soon

Puppy Patrol
King of the Castle

Jenny Dale

Illustrated by

Mick Reid

A Working Partners Book

MACMILLAN CHILDREN'S BOOKS

Special thanks to Cherith Baldry

First published 1999 by Macmillan Children's Books
a division of Macmillan Publishers Limited
25 Eccleston Place, London SW1W 9NF
and Basingstoke

Associated companies throughout the world

Created by Working Partners Limited
London W12 7QY

ISBN 0 330 37392 7

1 3 5 7 9 8 6 4 2

A CIP catalogue record for this book is available from
the British Library.

Typeset in Bookman Old Style by SX Composing DTP, Rayleigh, Essex
Printed and bound in Great Britain by Mackays of Chatham plc, Kent

Chapter One

Neil Parker stared into the blazing heart of the campfire and gently toasted a marshmallow on a long stick in the flickering heat.

Everything around him was dark. The only sounds were the crackling of the wood, the occasional cry of a night bird, and the soft plash of water from the nearby lake. A faint breeze stirred Neil's untidy brown hair and sent ripples through the grass.

"This is going to be a great holiday!" he said, smiling.

Neil's sister Emily grinned at him across the leaping flames of the fire. "The best ever," she added.

Neil patted Sam, his black and white Border collie, who lay contentedly beside him. "It'd be just perfect if Jake was here with us, too," Neil said. "Don't you think so, boy?"

Sam, who was Jake's dad, cocked his head to look at Neil, as if he agreed.

Neil pulled the toasted marshmallow from his stick, popped it into his mouth, and licked his sticky fingers. He felt full to bursting. Dirty plates from their meal of baked beans and sausages lay scattered around the fire, along with the dogs' food and water bowls.

"Jake's still too young to be away from home," Kate McGuire said. "Maybe in the summer."

It was the beginning of Neil and Emily's half-term holiday from school and they were taking a break from King Street Kennels, their home in the town of Compton, where their parents ran a boarding kennels and rescue centre. Kate, the Parkers' kennel maid, and her boyfriend Glen Paget had brought them for a week's camping in the Lake District.

Neil loved his home, and looking after the many different dogs who stayed at King Street. But it was exciting to be here, out in the open, with a whole week of swimming, hiking and exploring to look forward to – just as long as there was a dog or two to share it with.

"What about you, Julie?" Neil asked. "Are you missing Ben?"

Julie Baker, Emily's best friend, was poking a stick into the fire and watching the sparks fly upwards. When Neil spoke to her she looked wistful for a moment, and then giggled. "A bit," she admitted. "But he'd never fit into the camper van!"

Neil couldn't help grinning when he thought of her Old English sheepdog. Ben had a great personality, but he was huge – and possibly the clumsiest dog on earth.

"You can both phone home from the village

tomorrow," Kate promised, "and make sure everything's OK."

The campfire was starting to die down, while on the other side of the lake the moon was a bright crescent in the night sky. Neil traced a silver path stretching across the water to the lake shore where the camper van was parked with a large round tent pitched beside it. Further along the lake, half hidden by trees, he noticed the walls and towers of some enormous building which were outlined against the light.

Emily followed Neil's eyes and noticed the shape too.

"Is that a castle?"

"Yes," said Kate. "Ainsworth Castle, I think it's called."

Neil twisted round to give the dark walls a better look. "Can we go and see it?"

"Is it open to the public?" Julie added.

"I'm pretty sure it is," Glen said. "We'll check it out tomorrow."

"Great!" said Neil. "Do you remember when we recorded *The Time Travellers* in Padsham, Max?"

Max Hooper, the last of the camping party, was gazing into the fire distractedly. He was the star of the Parkers' favourite TV programme,

4

The Time Travellers, and had become friends with the family when an episode was recorded at Padsham Castle near Compton. He had just finished filming the last episode of the new series and was glad not to be working.

Max was absent-mindedly stroking Prince, his golden cocker spaniel who was, as Max always said, the real star of the show. Prince was dozing, sprawled across Max's feet like a silky rug.

Neil jabbed Max in the ribs. "Wake up, Max."

"Ainsworth Castle . . ." Max murmured. "That reminds me . . ." He straightened up and announced, "I've got some news!"

"News!" Emily ran her fingers through her short, dark hair, as she always did when she was excited. "I bet it's about *The Time Travellers*."

Max nodded.

"Tell us, Max," said Julie. "What is it?"

Max had a smug smile plastered all over his face and his eyes were shining.

"You're enjoying this, aren't you?" said Neil.

"Go on, tell us!" Emily begged.

"Well—" Max was just beginning, when a loud barking interrupted him.

Neil swivelled round and stared into the

gloom of the trees beside them that ran nearly as far as the water's edge. "That's a dog!"

"Full marks, Neil," said Emily.

Neil was already on his feet, with Sam standing alertly alongside him. Prince woke up and ran a few steps towards the lake barking in reply, his feathery tail waving frantically.

"Prince!" Max called, and reached out to grip his dog's collar as the cocker spaniel trotted back to him.

The unfamiliar barking came again, followed by the sound of something large pushing its way through the undergrowth along the lakeside.

"Here, boy!" Neil called.

Everyone was on their feet.

Glen took a couple of steps forward. "Can you see anything, Neil?"

A shape appeared from the bushes and stood near the water's edge. It was a tall, rangy dog with a sleek coat that seemed to shine silver in the moonlight.

"Wow!" breathed Emily.

"Is it real?" whispered Julie.

There was something unearthly about the dog. It looked almost like a reflection shimmering on the surface of the lake. Neil's common sense pushed the odd feeling aside as he looked closer. "That's a Weimaraner, isn't it?" he said.

"Yes, and it's a beauty," Kate replied.

"But what's it doing here?" asked Emily. "Where's its owner?"

"Maybe it's lost," said Julie.

Neil got up and approached the strange dog.

"Be careful," Glen warned him.

Neil nodded and slowly, so as not to startle it, he held out a hand to the dog. It sniffed his finger delicately and then pushed its muzzle up against him, demanding his attention. Neil slipped it a dog treat from the supply he always carried in his pocket.

"Wouldn't you know!" said Emily. "Neil doesn't even have to go looking for dogs. He just sits there, and they come to him!"

Grinning, Neil patted the animal. "She's a beauty, isn't she?"

The dog followed him back to the campfire and lay down next to him on the opposite side from Sam. Her tongue hung out as if she was really pleased with herself. When Max released Prince, the cocker spaniel came and gave her a friendly sniff, and the Weimaraner nosed him calmly.

In the firelight, Neil could see that her coat

was steely grey, and her eyes, amber. Neil drew his hand down the dog's sleek neck. "She's not wearing a collar," he said. "What's your name, girl?"

Glen walked over to the bushes where the dog had first appeared. "Hello!" he called. "Anyone there?"

No one replied.

"It's after ten," Kate said, as Glen came back to the fire, shrugging. "Too late to be walking your dog. Maybe she escaped from somewhere."

"She's been well looked after," said Neil. "You can see she's been properly fed and groomed. Somebody must be missing her."

"Well, it's too late to do anything tonight," Kate replied. She yawned and stretched. "We'll look for her owners in the morning. It's time to clean up and go to bed now. Girls in the camper van, boys in the tent, OK?"

Reluctantly, everyone got up and started to collect the plates and pans from the meal.

Neil groaned as he picked up a pan crusted with baked beans, took it down to the lakeside, and started sloshing it around in the water.

Max followed with a handful of plates and squatted down beside him. "It's too dark for this," he said. "I vote we leave it till the morning."

"I'm for that," Neil agreed. "And we haven't heard your news, either."

Max gave him the smug smile again. "It'll keep till breakfast."

Neil filled the pan and left it at the water's edge. Stifling yawns, they started to walk towards the tent. Before they reached it, the roar of a car engine shattered the peace of the night. A moment later, two powerful headlights angled round a bend and swept across the campsite. Neil threw up an arm as the light shone into his eyes and blinded him. Both Sam and Prince started barking.

"Whassat?" gasped Neil.

Kate scrambled to her feet, and Glen stuck his head out of the tent.

The vehicle – a large Range Rover – pulled up beside the camper van. The driver cut the engine and got out. He opened the back of the car and let out one of the biggest dogs that Neil had ever seen.

Neil was so fascinated by it that he didn't pay much attention to the man. The dog was huge, with a deep chest and slender legs. The colour of the coat was hard to make out in the poor light; Neil thought it was fawn. It stood with its elegant head raised, looking at the group round the fire.

"Great Dane!" Neil said to Max. "He's fantastic!"

The dog's owner planted himself on the edge of the firelight and looked round. "Who's in charge here?" he asked, his voice raised to make himself heard over the barking of the dogs. "Stop that racket, can't you?"

Neil and Max went to their dogs and calmed them down. Emily made a face at Neil and muttered, "It was quiet before he came."

"I wonder what he wants," Julie said nervously.

Neil stayed crouched beside Sam, a hand on his neck, and looked up at the newcomer. He was a tall man, with greying hair and a bristling moustache. He wore a tweed suit and carried a stick. "Well?" he snapped.

He looked as if he was used to having his orders obeyed right away.

"We're in charge, I suppose," said Kate, glancing across at Glen.

The man looked from one to the other and snorted. "And do you know you're on my land?"

Glen crawled out of the tent and stood up,

brushing at his jeans and tossing back his long, floppy hair. "Are we really? I'm sorry. I looked at the map and I thought—"

"Then you *thought* wrong. This is my property and I don't welcome campers."

Kate and Glen started apologizing again.

Neil went to make friends with the Great Dane. The owner might be causing problems, but that was no reason to ignore his dog.

The Great Dane's noble-looking head almost reached Neil's shoulders; he lowered it and sniffed interestedly as Neil held out a hand.

Neil patted him and stroked the smooth, triangular ears.

"Hello, boy," he said, fishing in his pocket for a titbit. "You're great—"

"Leave that dog alone!" It was the owner's voice again.

"It's all right," Neil said. "I know about dogs. My mum and dad run a kennels, and I—"

"Rubbish!" the man said irritably.

"No, it's true, sir," Max spoke up. "Neil's an expert. He helped me when I had a problem with my dog." He gestured towards Prince, who was quiet again and wagging his tail hopefully as if he wanted to be friends.

The man's eyebrows shot up. "That dog!"

For a minute Neil thought that he had recognized Prince from *The Time Travellers*. Then he realized that the man was staring fixedly beyond Prince at the Weimaraner.

"That does it!" he exploded. "Take yourselves and your dogs off my land – right away!"

Chapter Two

"We're not doing any harm," Neil protested.

The landowner leant on his stick and looked Neil up and down. "You seem to have a lot to say for yourself, young man."

Neil shuffled his feet uncomfortably.

The man shrugged and turned back to Kate and Glen. "You're trespassing on my land. You've pitched a tent, lit a fire – and let your animals run free."

Neil looked at the dogs. Prince was standing very close to Max, as if he knew something was wrong and didn't like it. The Weimaraner was lying down, head raised, and Sam was sitting alongside her with an alert expression. None of them was tied up – but they weren't running free, either.

"They are under control," Neil spluttered.

The man ignored him. "I don't want you here," he said to Glen, "and I'm asking you to leave. Now."

"But look." It was Kate who replied. "We've got four children here. And we can't organize anywhere else to go at this time of night."

Julie was looking scared, but Neil could see that Emily was boiling with indignation. Suddenly, she spoke. "It's the Weimaraner, isn't it?"

"What?" the man responded. "What are you talking about?"

"It's the Weimaraner." Emily looked determined. "When you saw her you looked surprised – and got even angrier."

"She's not our dog," Glen started to explain. "She's only just turned up. Do you know who owns her?"

"No. Why should I know about every wretched mongrel straying on my land?"

"Mongrel?" Neil spluttered. "That's a pure-bred Weimaraner. If you don't know that, then you're the one who doesn't know about dogs!"

"Neil!" Glen made frantic hand movements

14

and tried to calm Neil down. "We're very sorry to have strayed onto your land by accident, but would you let us stay here just for tonight?"

The man glanced from Emily, Julie and Max by the fire, to Neil, standing by his own Great Dane, and then back to Kate and Glen. "Well . . ."

"We'll make sure everything is cleared up," added Glen. "You won't know we've been here."

The man nodded curtly. "Very well. But please make sure you are gone first thing tomorrow or I'll call the police. Goodnight to you."

He turned and stalked off back towards the Range Rover. As he passed the Great Dane he slapped his stick against his leg, and snapped, "King – heel!"

The massive dog turned obediently and climbed into the back of the Range Rover again. His owner turned it round with some difficulty in the narrow space and roared off up the track, disappearing into the blackness.

"What a horrible man," Emily muttered.

"Horrible man or not," Glen said regretfully, "we'd better turn in. There's a lot to do tomorrow."

15

"We've got to find the Weimaraner's owner," said Neil.

Glen poured water on the remains of the fire. "And somewhere else to stay."

Without the light and warmth of the flames the campsite suddenly seemed unfriendly. A chill wind was blowing off the lake. When everyone had moved away from the steaming fire, Neil was left looking into the darkness, where King had been standing.

"I love Great Danes," said Emily, coming to stand beside him. The Weimaraner was with her.

"Yeah, nice dog – shame about the owner." Neil stroked the Weimaraner's head.

"I wonder . . ." Emily frowned.

"Wonder what?" asked Neil.

"What it was about the Weimaraner that made King's owner so angry."

Neil shook his head, sighed, then decided to retire to the tent. Whatever it was would have to wait until the next day. He was exhausted.

Sunlight glittered on the lake the next morning as Neil and the others sat eating breakfast by the water's edge.

"Where should we go?" Neil asked, chasing

scrambled egg around his plate with a piece of bread.

"I don't know." Glen looked worried. "I was sure this was common land. I suppose we could try the official campsites, but they'll be expensive."

"And full," Kate said, as everyone began to put things away. "I tell you what, Neil. Why don't Glen and I clear up here, while the rest of you take the Weimaraner into the village and try to find her owner. We'll meet you in the square at, say, midday?"

"Sure," said Neil. Leaving Kate and Glen to begin packing up, he crawled into the tent and fished out a backpack from his scattered possessions.

"What's that for?" Max asked, as he joined him and neatly rolled up his sleeping bag.

"Dog emergency kit," Neil explained. He waved a plastic box and stuffed it into the backpack. "First aid stuff. And the water bowls. And water. It's going to be a hot day, so we'll have to be careful the dogs don't overheat."

Max nodded. Neil had thought of everything.

Five minutes later, Neil and the others set off for the nearby village of Beckthwaite. The narrow

17

track joined the road that skirted the lake and led through the village. Once they had reached it, Neil and Max clipped leads on Sam and Prince. Neil was worried that they had no lead for the Weimaraner, but she walked obediently at heel, as if she was perfectly trained and well used to roads and traffic.

The sun was beating down. As they approached the outskirts of Beckthwaite, Neil could feel sweat trickling down his back under his T-shirt. "Let's see if we can find a café," he suggested. "We can get a cold drink, and ask about the dog."

Everyone thought that was a good idea. Sam barked in agreement, and Prince wagged his tail excitedly. "Yes, drinks for you too!" Neil promised.

The road quickly became the village high street. Small grey houses with slate roofs huddled together on the slope of the hill to the left, while to the right, through the trees, they caught glimpses of the castle battlements.

Beckthwaite high street was lined with shops selling hiking gear, food and souvenirs. The pavements were crowded with visitors in shirts, shorts and sunhats, so Neil and the others had to weave their way in single file and keep the dogs close beside them.

Eventually they stopped outside a café with a brightly painted sign above the window.

Neil looked up. "Beckthwaite Bakery. This should do."

"Great," said Julie. "I'm parched."

They piled in through the door. The café was gloriously cool after the baking hot street outside. Behind the counter there were shelves of bread and buns, while further back were tables and chairs where a few people were enjoying tea or cold drinks.

A plump, grey-haired woman was standing behind the counter. "Hey!" she said. "You can't bring those dogs in here."

Neil halted, looked round and stared at her. "But there are dogs in here already," he objected, pointing to where a Border collie like Sam was lying at the feet of an old man sitting at one of the tables.

The woman flushed slightly. "I know that dog. He's well-behaved.

"But ours are too—" Emily protested.

"Go on, clear off, the lot of you, before I call the police."

"Why—" Emily started, but Neil put a hand gently on her shoulder and she was quiet.

One or two of the people at the tables turned to see what was going on. They didn't look friendly either.

Neil shrugged. "OK, we'll go," he said. "But we weren't doing any harm."

The woman watched them suspiciously as they retreated through the door and moved off down the street.

"What did we do?" asked Julie, puzzled.

"Rattled her cage, I think." Max tried to smile.

"Well, we've got to keep trying," said Emily. She patted the Weimaraner's silky neck. "Otherwise we'll never find her owner. I'll get us some drinks from the newsagent's."

"Good idea," said Neil. He waited outside with Max and Julie. Sam and Prince flopped down at their feet, panting, while the Weimaraner stood and calmly watched the passers-by.

A woman walking along with a loaded shopping basket came to a halt when she saw them, then very pointedly crossed the street so she didn't have to walk past them.

"Did you see that?" asked Neil. "You'd think we'd got the plague."

"Maybe she doesn't like dogs," said Max.

Neil began to feel as if everybody in the village was staring at him, and he was glad when

Emily reappeared. She was carrying a selection of canned drinks and several small slabs of Kendal mint cake.

Still shaking their heads they walked on to the cobbled village square. Everyone sank down thankfully on the steps of the market cross in the centre and shared out the food and drink.

"This place is mad," said Julie.

Neil nodded and unhitched his backpack. He took out some bowls and a bottle of water to give the dogs a drink. The Weimaraner waited until Sam had finished, and then had a drink from his bowl.

Emily cracked open a can and looked round. Across the square, beyond a church with a spire, was a pub called the Ainsworth Arms. Outside, beside a wooden bench, was a young woman with a large black Labrador sat at her feet. "You know," she said suddenly, finishing off a generous swig from her can. "I think it was the Weimaraner, again."

"What do you mean?" asked Neil.

"Well, last night that man got really furious when he saw her. And now the people here are acting unfriendly. I think it's because she's with us. There's nothing so unusual about us otherwise." She put her hands on either side of the Weimaraner's muzzle and looked into her eyes. "And you're such a beauty, aren't you, girl?"

"Why on earth would anyone take a dislike to such a lovely dog?" Julie added.

"If she is local she might be able to lead us to somebody who knows where she lives," Neil said.

The Weimaraner, who had been sitting contentedly at the foot of the steps, suddenly got to her feet, and stood looking alertly up at Neil. Then she walked away a few paces, stopped, and waited.

"She wants you to follow her!" said Julie.

"Maybe she does." Neil drained his can and tossed it in the nearest litter bin. "OK, girl, lead the way."

The dog set off back the way they had come. Neil and the others followed. When they came to a narrow lane leading to Ainsworth Castle, she turned into it. The lane twisted through trees and shrubs, then crossed a grassy space that led down to the lakeside. Neil halted and stared. "Wow!" he said. "Look at that!"

Just opposite, a solid stone causeway jutted out into the lake. At the other end was Ainsworth Castle – grey walls and towers mirrored in the quiet water. The windows were narrow slits. A few visitors passed along the causeway and under the iron portcullis in the arched gateway.

Max spread his arms. "Brilliant!" he said, spinning round to face them. "It's Camelot!"

Neil looked at the others and tapped his forehead. "Mad."

"No, seriously! That's the news I was going to tell you last night. There's going to be a feature film of *The Time Travellers*. Zeno and Prince are going back to the time of King Arthur and his knights of the round table."

"A film!" Julie exclaimed.

"Max, that's great!" said Emily.

"No wonder you were looking so pleased with yourself," added Neil.

"The problem is," Max went on, "they haven't found a suitable castle yet that they could use for Camelot. But I think this one would be perfect!"

"Why don't you ask the owner, then?" Neil suggested. "And we can ask about the Weimaraner at the same time. After all, she brought us here."

"Have we got enough money to go in?" Emily asked, looking at the admission charges listed on a large noticeboard nearby.

Julie glanced at her watch. "Yes, but I don't think we've got enough time. We're supposed to be meeting Kate and Glen in half an hour."

"Well, perhaps we can do the guided tour another time," Neil said. "But right now, I'm going to find somebody I can ask about this dog."

Emily grabbed his arm. "Neil, I think that would be a *really* bad idea." She jerked her thumb towards the causeway.

Neil looked to where she was pointing. From underneath the portcullis, King the Great Dane emerged and began walking proudly across the causeway. He was guided by a girl of about eleven, Neil's age, with long fair hair and a thin, waspish face.

Behind them, waving his stick, was the man who had visited their camp the night before. He looked furious.

Chapter Three

The man strode across the stone causeway to where Neil and the others were standing. "I thought I told you to get off my land!" he barked.

"We're not on your land," Neil retorted. "This is a public road, isn't it?"

"No, it's a private road." The man's face reddened. "I don't want you or your dogs anywhere near my property. Go back where you came from, and take that . . . thing with you." He gestured with his stick towards the Weimaraner.

"We keep telling you," said Emily, "she's not *our* dog. We thought she might belong to the owner of the castle."

"Oh, did you? Well, young lady, I'm Lord Ainsworth and the castle belongs to me. And I can assure you that this is not my dog. Now, go."

Shrugging, Neil looked round for Max and Julie. Somehow he felt it would be a bad time for Max to ask if he could use the castle for a film set. He was about to call Max when he noticed a woman with two children, both a bit younger than Emily, stop on their way into the castle. They looked carefully at Max and then at each other. One of the children whispered something to his mother. She went up to Max and asked, "Excuse me, are you Max Hooper?"

Max looked embarrassed. "Yes, I am," he replied.

"And that's Prince!" the little girl exclaimed. She and her brother both crouched down to pet the cocker spaniel. Prince's long, feathery tail waved enthusiastically as he revelled in all the attention.

"Please," the little boy said to Max, "would you give us your autograph? We always watch *The Time Travellers*!"

The children's mother fished a piece of paper out of her handbag. Max took it and signed his name. One or two other people stopped to look, and soon he was in the middle of a little knot of excited fans. Neil grinned. "The price of fame," he said.

Lord Ainsworth was looking irritable. "Would someone please tell me what's going on?"

The Great Dane, along with the unfriendly-looking girl, had come up beside him. The girl was watching Max curiously, but she said nothing.

"That's Max Hooper," Emily volunteered. "You've probably seen him on TV. He's the star of *The Time Travellers*."

Lord Ainsworth snorted contemptuously.

"A lot of people like it," Neil pointed out. "You don't want to be the man who threw the star of *The Time Travellers* – and his famous dog – off your land, do you?"

For a minute he thought Lord Ainsworth might explode. Then he let out a long breath. "Young man, you're far too clever for your own good."

"I'm sorry," Neil said. "We don't mean any harm, honestly. We're only trying to help this dog. You should understand that – especially when you've got such a smashing dog yourself." He turned to the Great Dane. "Hello, King. Do you remember me?"

Lord Ainsworth seemed to relax a little. Not many owners could stay angry if you praised their dogs. Neil fondled King's ears and offered him a dog treat. But as he smiled down at the dog, Neil froze, as he caught sight of King's eyes.

King was blinking repeatedly, his eyes watering, as if he'd got some grit or dust in them. Neil looked closer, but he could see nothing. "What's the matter with his eyes?" he asked.

"What?" Lord Ainsworth started. "Nothing."

"But there is. You can see they're watering."

"Hmm – touch of cold, maybe."

"Possibly, but I don't think so," Neil replied. He bent to get as close to King's eyes as he could. King stood still and gazed up at him steadily.

Neil was trying to remember what Mike Turner, the Compton vet, had once said about a Great Dane who was boarding at King Street Kennels. Something about his eyelids . . .

"Oh, yes, you're the dog expert. Well, young man—"

"I think you should take him to the vet," Neil said, not really listening. "If this is what I think it is, then King could go blind."

He heard a gasp from the fair-haired girl who was still holding King's lead. Neil looked up at her, but still she said nothing. Lord Ainsworth snatched the lead out of her hand.

"Do you think I can't look after my own dog?" he snapped and led King away. The dog went with him obediently as he stalked back across the causeway and disappeared beneath the portcullis.

As Neil watched him go, he couldn't help admiring the Great Dane even more for the patience he showed when he must be suffering badly. "I wasn't joking, you know," he repeated to the girl. "I think your dog might go blind if he doesn't get proper treatment."

"Neil knows what he's talking about," Emily added. "Our mum and dad run a boarding kennels, so we see a lot of dogs."

"It's a condition that Great Danes get," Neil explained. "Our vet told me what it's called, but I can't remember the name. A dog at the kennels had it. Their eyelids turn inwards, so the lashes scratch the eyeball and the dog feels really uncomfortable. It needs an operation or the eyes can be permanently damaged."

The girl looked at Neil and Emily as if she

wasn't sure whether she wanted to talk to them or not.

"I'm Neil," Neil said, trying to be friendly. "This is my sister Emily, and our friend Julie." Sam woofed as if he didn't want to be left out. "Oh, yes," Neil added, grinning. "And this is Sam."

"Hello, Sam." The girl bent down and played with Sam's ears. She seemed to find it easier to talk to dogs rather than people. "I'm Penny Ainsworth," she told Neil. "Lord Ainsworth is my father. Is your other friend really Max Hooper?"

Neil managed to stop himself saying he felt sorry for anyone who had Lord Ainsworth as a father. He glanced over at Max, who was just saying goodbye to the last of his fans. He strolled back towards Neil and the others, with Prince at his heels.

"Hi there, superstar," Neil said. "Here's another fan of yours. This is Penny Ainsworth. Lord Ainsworth is her dad." He nodded significantly across to the castle.

"Oh, so that's the man who—" Max closed his mouth on whatever he had been about to say. "Hello, Penny."

"I really like your programme," Penny said shyly. She had gone pink but at least she was smiling a little.

"Thank you," said Max.

"We all love it," Emily said.

Neil nodded. "Max, tell her about the film."

Max repeated the plans to make a film set in the court of King Arthur, and how the production team were looking for a castle to use as Camelot. "And I thought," he said, gesturing towards the towers of Ainsworth Castle, "this would be just perfect."

Penny listened open-mouthed. She let out her breath in a long sigh. "Oh, it would be wonderful!" Then gradually her unhappy look came back. "But it's no use. Daddy would never allow it."

"Why not?" Neil asked, amazed.

Penny shrugged. "It's just how he is. He doesn't approve of films and TV. He likes tradition and doesn't like change." She hesitated, and then went on. "That's why he's so funny about King. You see, King is descended from the boarhounds that the lords of the castle here used for hunting in the Middle Ages."

"Though the breed's about four thousand years old," added Neil knowledgeably.

Penny Ainsworth continued. "That's right, and the Lord of Ainsworth Castle has always kept one of them as his special companion. There's a legend that if the line of Great Danes is ever broken, then the Lord of Ainsworth will have no heir, and Ainsworth Castle will fall into the lake."

Neil and Emily gave each other a blank look. Max suppressed a smile.

"But that doesn't make sense," said Neil. "If your dad really believes that old story, then he should be *looking after* King."

Penny shrugged again, looking even more

33

unhappy. "I don't know if he really believes it. But when—" She stopped herself, and this time she didn't go on.

"Well, whether he believes it or not," Neil said, "he ought to get a vet to look at King. He's your father – can't you persuade him?"

"We'll help if we can," said Emily.

"It's difficult to get him to change his mind." Penny went red again. "I know you think he's horrible and I'm sorry he was rude to you. He's not *always* like that."

Neil interrupted them. "You've got to have King examined! If you care about him. He's suffering, you know."

Penny suddenly looked furious. "Do you think I don't care? But it's not just King – there are other problems that you know nothing about. You don't understand! You don't understand anything!"

Stifling a sob, she turned and ran back towards the castle gateway. Neil stared after her. "What's got into her?"

"She's upset about King, you can see," said Julie.

"And something else," said Emily.

Max murmured agreement. "I feel sorry for her."

"OK," said Neil. "I'd feel sorry for anyone with a dad like that. But what I want to know is, what are we going to do to help King?"

Chapter Four

Penny had stopped under the archway and was talking to a smart man wearing an official-looking blazer. He looked as if he was calming her down. Then Penny disappeared and the man strode quickly across the causeway towards Neil and the others.

"Now what?" said Neil.

But the newcomer was smiling as he approached. He was about the same age as Neil's dad, with fair hair and a thin, beaky face. He wore gold-rimmed spectacles.

"Hello," he said. "I'm Adrian Bartlett, Lord Ainsworth's steward. I gather from Penny that there's been a bit of a problem?"

"I'm sorry if we upset her," Emily said.

Mr Bartlett scratched his head. "Don't worry. I'm sure it's not your fault. What's all this about King's eyes?"

Neil told him who they were, and how they had experience with dogs. He described what he thought was the matter with the Great Dane.

"Hmm . . ." said Mr Bartlett. "I'd noticed his eyes were watering. But I don't know the first thing about dogs. I'm a cat man myself. I'll have a word with Lord Ainsworth," he promised. "Tactfully. When he's in a good mood."

"Oh, he does have good moods?" The words were out before Neil could stop them. He felt himself going red, and Emily elbowed him in the ribs. "Sorry," he apologized. "That was rude of me."

"Well," said Mr Bartlett, "Lord Ainsworth has problems you know nothing about. Give him a break, hmm?"

Neil nodded. "It's just that every time we see him, he shouts at us. He seemed to take a dislike to us from the first time he set eyes on us."

"It's this dog," Emily said, pointing to the Weimaraner, who had been sitting calmly beside her. "I don't think Lord Ainsworth likes her. And she's not even ours."

Adrian Bartlett's eyebrows climbed up into his hair. "I'm not surprised. That dog belongs to the travellers."

"Who?" Neil asked. Emily and Julie exchanged delighted smiles. It looked as if they had found out something about the Weimaraner's owners at last.

"Travellers," said Mr Bartlett. "Gypsies. They've been camping along the lakeside for the last few weeks. I've seen them in Beckthwaite several times, and that dog was with them."

"So lots of the villagers must have seen her as well," Max said. "They must have thought we were with the gypsies. That's why they kept moving us on."

"It's no excuse," said Emily. "We hadn't done anything."

Adrian Bartlett shook his head. "A lot of people don't like gypsies just *because* they're gypsies. And to be fair, other types of travellers *have* caused problems here in the past. Fences damaged, gates left open – and you know what problems that can cause in the country. Last year, one of Lord Ainsworth's tenant farmers had to have a prize cow put down because it wandered into the road and was hit by a car."

Emily bent down to pat the Weimaraner. "I

can't believe they're that bad when they've got such a lovely dog. She's really gentle and well-trained."

"Well, maybe these Romany gypsies are OK," said Mr Bartlett. "I'd give them the benefit of the doubt, myself, but a lot of people won't."

"Now we know who owns her," Neil said, "we ought to take her back. You said the gypsies are camped beside the lake?"

"You'll see the turn-off about a mile outside the village," Mr Bartlett told him. "It's a large group – probably about fifteen or so caravans in all. I think I recognize them from last autumn."

Neil nodded. "We'll go straight away."

Adrian Bartlett frowned. "Be careful about going there by yourselves. Aren't your parents with you?"

Neil explained about Kate and Glen.

Mr Bartlett smiled. "I hope you have a better holiday from now on. Do come back and visit the castle if you get the chance."

He raised a hand and was turning back towards the castle entrance when Max said, "Who would I ask about using the castle for a film?"

"A film?" Adrian Bartlett stopped and looked puzzled. When Neil had introduced Max, Mr

39

Bartlett had obviously not connected him with *The Time Travellers*. "Well, to begin with, you would ask me, as I'm Lord Ainsworth's steward. That means I'm his business manager. But of course, Lord Ainsworth would have to agree."

A beaming smile lit up Mr Bartlett's face as Max began to explain about the King Arthur film.

"Ainsworth castle as Camelot! That would be wonderful." He spun round and stared at the castle, dreamily. "Knights in armour. Fluttering banners . . . horses . . . fair ladies . . ." He coughed and added more practically, "We could certainly use the money."

He took a deep breath and faced Neil and the others again. "Look, Max . . . I can't promise anything. But I'll see what Lord Ainsworth has to say. Will you be around for a while?"

"Until the end of the week," Max said. "But I'll give Brian Mason a ring at Prince Productions in Manchester. He's the director of *The Time Travellers* and he's responsible for choosing the locations."

"Great!" He fumbled in his pocket and pulled out a slightly tatty business card. "Here's my number. If he gets in touch with me, I'll arrange for him to come and have a look."

"That's ace!" said Max, and Prince barked in agreement.

"And now I really must get back to work. Let me know how you get on with the gypsies."

"We will," said Neil. "And you won't forget about King?"

"His eyes? No, I promise." Adrian Bartlett said goodbye and walked quickly back across the causeway.

"He's nice," said Julie.

"Except he likes cats," muttered Neil. "Who would want cats when there's a great dog like King around?"

"And what did he mean, they could use the

money?" Emily asked. She spread her arms. "How can you be short of money when you've got all this?"

Neil and the others hurried back to the centre of Beckthwaite where they had arranged to meet Kate and Glen. It was well after midday and the white camper van was already parked there when they arrived. Glen was sunning himself on the steps of the market cross, but there was no sign of Kate.

"Hi," Glen said. "No luck with the Weimaraner?"

Neil explained what Adrian Bartlett had told them about the gypsies. "So we'd better take her back to them," he finished.

"And then maybe people will stop being nasty to us," said Julie.

"OK," said Glen. "We'll go as soon as Kate gets back. She went to the tourist office to ask about campsites."

"While we're waiting," Neil said, "can we phone home? There's a phone box over there."

Max and Julie phoned home too, before Kate appeared from a doorway on the other side of the square. Her usually cheerful face was depressed, strands of long, fair hair were coming

42

out of her ponytail, and she looked tired as she flopped down on the steps beside Glen.

"Everywhere's full," she said. "I don't know where we're going to sleep tonight."

Glen put an arm round her shoulders and gave her a hug.

"It's not all bad news, Kate. We found the Weimaraner's owners," said Emily.

"That's good." Kate's smile reappeared. "So why is she still here?"

"Because we have to take her home." Glen sprang to his feet. "Right, folks, here's what we do. One, find the gypsy camp and return the dog. Two, have lunch. Fish and chips on me, OK?"

"OK," said Neil. Sam barked loudly.

"And dog food, Sam," Glen said, laughing. "You've not been forgotten. Three, find somewhere to stay. All in favour?"

Five hands waved enthusiastically. Sam and Prince wagged their tails.

"Right," said Glen. "Into the van, everybody!"

Driving out of the village with Glen at the wheel, they passed the turning for Ainsworth Castle, and then the track that led to their old campsite. A little further on a third lane led through woodland to the lakeshore. As Glen turned into it, he said, "You know, I think this is the road I was looking for last night. According to the map it leads down to common land beside the lake."

"Maybe we can stay here too," Emily suggested.

"We'll see."

The road emerged out of the trees into a clearing. Glen pulled up the camper van on the edge of a large semicircle of caravans. Mostly they were a ragged assortment of old and slightly newer mobile homes, but three of the caravans stood out. They were real Romany caravans, made of wood and brightly painted in scarlet and yellow and blue. Their rounded roofs had scalloped edges and even the wheels and shafts were patterned.

Behind the caravans horses were grazing, and one or two mongrel dogs were wandering around in the open space. In the middle of the semicircle a fire blazed up. Two or three people squatted around it, and looked up as the camper van appeared. Neil almost felt as though he had stepped back a hundred years, until he noticed that one of the boys by the fire was listening to a Walkman.

44

One of the gypsies, a tall man wearing black trousers and a bright shirt, rose and came towards them.

Glen got down from the driver's seat; Neil scrambled after him and Emily followed, coaxing the Weimaraner.

"Hello," Glen said. "I think we've found your dog."

The man looked at the Weimaraner, grunted something, and turned back to the fire. "Keziah!" he called.

A striking-looking woman got up and walked across to the van. Neil couldn't tell how old she was. She was unusually tall, with bright black eyes in a brown face. Her hair was long and dark, tied in a yellow scarf. Heavy gold jewellery flashed at her ears, neck and wrists.

Once the Weimaraner saw her, she trotted over to her side, turned, and came back with her as she approached the van.

The woman let a hand rest on the dog's head. "*Sarishan*," she said to Glen. "Be welcome. I see my dog has found you."

"Well, I suppose . . ." Glen looked a bit embarrassed, as if he hadn't expected the woman to say that.

"Yes, she did." Neil suddenly felt excited. "At

least, she was wandering around by the lake where we were camping last night."

"I can see she's yours," Emily said, smiling as she watched the Weimaraner sitting contentedly at the gypsy woman's feet.

"Thank you." The woman's brown face creased into an answering smile. "My name is Keziah Lee. You are welcome to our camp. We have much to talk about."

"Well, that's kind of you, Mrs Lee," said Glen, "but we can't stay. We have to look for somewhere to camp, for one thing. Now the dog's back where she belongs—"

"We have much to talk about," Keziah

repeated, interrupting him. Glen glanced uncertainly at Kate, who got down from the van and stood beside him. Max and Julie scrambled out too.

"This dog," said Keziah, "knows what the future will bring. She found you and led you to me. And to do that she must have had a reason."

"And we have to find out what it is!" Emily exclaimed. Neil looked perplexed.

"Yes," Keziah said. She glanced round the circle of faces. "Something important is about to happen. You and I and the dog will discover what it is, and decide what we must do."

Chapter Five

Glen and Kate stared at each other. "Now look, Mrs Lee," Glen said, "she's a lovely dog, but honestly, isn't that all a bit far-fetched?"

Keziah laughed. "I can see what you're thinking. Maybe this ignorant gypsy woman says these things so we cross her palm with silver to tell our fortunes."

Glen went scarlet. "I don't think that at all. But dogs that see into the future . . . come on!"

Keziah's eyes were crinkled with amusement; she was not a bit offended by what Glen had said. She gestured towards the caravan in the centre of the semicircle; it was the biggest and most brightly painted of them all. "This is my *vardo*. Come, sit with me," she invited.

She nodded at the man in black who had called her, and he inclined his head before going back to whatever he was doing by the fire. He almost bowed to her, Neil thought. Just as if she was a queen!

Keziah seated herself on the top step of the caravan with the Weimaraner beside her. Everyone else crowded in on the steps below. Kate introduced herself and the rest of their party.

"Tell us about the dog," Emily begged.

"Her name is Chavi," said Keziah. "That is a Romany word for girl. She came to us in the night."

"What do you mean?" Julie asked breathlessly.

"One night, two summers ago," said Keziah, "when I was asleep in my *vardo*, the whining of a dog woke me up. At first I thought it was one of our own dogs, but in the end I went out to look."

"What did you see?" Max leant forward. "Was it Chavi?"

"It was. She was sitting at the foot of the steps. The moon was shining on her. When she saw the door open she came in."

"And you never found her owners?" Neil asked.

Keziah looked amused. "Maybe we did not try very hard. But I believe that Chavi chose to come to us. And ever since then she has been able to tell us what will happen. Sometimes she tells us what we must do. She led us here to the lake where we intend to spend summer."

She smiled at Glen, who was still looking doubtful. "Once, not long after she came," Keziah went on, "we were going to make camp by a river. Chavi sat and barked, right where I wanted to prepare my *vardo*. When she would not stop, we camped further up the hill, even though it was a long way to carry the water." Her voice dropped to a whisper. "That night it rained, and the river burst its banks. If we had camped there, all would have been swept away."

"Coincidence," said Glen.

Kate prodded him and looked embarrassed.

"OK! I give in!" He stretched down and stroked Chavi's sleek neck. "She's certainly a beautiful dog."

Neil said nothing, but he couldn't help thinking that it was all very hard to believe. Emily and Julie, though, were drinking in the story with shining eyes.

"Can we come and walk her while we're staying here?" Emily asked. "We'd take really good care of her."

"Of course," said Keziah.

"Hang on a minute," said Kate. "We don't know where we'll be tomorrow. We still have to find somewhere to sleep tonight."

"Is that all? Along this stretch of the lake is all common land," Keziah said. She rose and pointed in the opposite direction from the castle. "There's plenty of room for you to camp."

"That's such a relief!" said Glen.

"It's certainly a load off our minds," Kate agreed. "I was afraid we'd have to park in a lay-by somewhere."

"Then go and make your camp," Keziah said, "and come back this evening for a meal with us. We will show you how the Rom feast."

"The Rom?" Max asked. "What's that?"

"We are the Rom." Keziah swept a hand to take in all the camp and its occupants. "You call us gypsies or travellers, but the Rom is what we call ourselves; true Romanies who live our lives by the old ways. Tradition is dear to us, as is the countryside. We respect it, and all who use her sensibly."

"Can we go, Kate? Please?" said Neil.

"Yes, it's very kind of Keziah," said Kate. "We'd love to, wouldn't we?"

Keziah smiled and showed Glen the track where he could drive the van closer to their new camping place. She stood with a hand on Chavi's head as Neil and the others said goodbye.

"I like Keziah," Emily said, as she scrambled back into the camper van. "And I love Chavi! I'm going to walk her tomorrow. Are you coming, Julie?"

"Sure," said Julie. "And maybe we'll find out what she wants us to do."

That evening, the Romany camp became a mysterious and exciting place. The only light came from the central fire, the flames glancing on the bright paint of the caravans and illuminating the dark circle of trees beyond. Neil felt a shiver down his spine. All this, and a dog with second sight too!

A huge pot was bubbling on the fire, sending out enticing smells. Neil realized how hungry he was. It had been a very long day.

As he and the others entered the camp, Keziah came to meet them. Firelight gleamed on her gold ornaments. *"Sarishan*, my friends," she said.

"Sarishan, Keziah," said Emily shyly.

Keziah gave her a brilliant smile. "Soon you will speak Rom like one of us!"

She showed them where they could sit close to the fire, and soon the other gypsies brought round bowls of the delicious-smelling stew.

"You know, Em," Neil said, "none of this would have happened without Chavi. She's the best!"

The meal was drawing to an end. Neil felt that he couldn't eat another mouthful. He let Sam finish off the remains of the stew in his bowl and leant back against the tree to look up at the stars. Beside him, Emily was drowsing, with Chavi lying between her and Julie. On Neil's other side Max sat with his arms wrapped round his knees. Prince was sprawled beside him.

"This couldn't be better," Max said.

"Except for King," Neil reminded him. "Tomorrow I'm going to see Penny and Mr Bartlett, and see if they've spoken to Lord Ainsworth yet."

"I wonder if—" Max broke off at the sound of

loud voices and laughter from the other side of the fire.

"Hey, *boshengro!*" someone shouted.

One of the gypsies got to his feet with a violin in his hands. He was tall and dark with a shock of curly hair, and he wore a checked shirt. Somehow Neil thought he looked familiar, though he didn't remember seeing the young man when they first visited the camp.

The man tucked the violin under his chin and began to play. The music was fast and lively, and the voices died away until there was no other sound. Emily sat up and listened, bright-eyed.

"He's good," said Max, tapping his feet in time to the music.

The young violinist had his head bent over his instrument, his hair hiding his face. He seemed to be putting everything he had into his music. At last he ended with a flourish and stood for a moment with head thrown back, panting as if he had run a race.

Emily started to clap; Neil and Max joined in, and the violinist glanced at them briefly, nodded, then sat down again among his people by the fire. He hadn't looked pleased to be applauded.

"Maybe we did something wrong," said Emily.

"No." Keziah spoke from behind her. She had approached so silently that no one had heard her. "*Boshengro*, he is touchy and little pleases him. He is a recent arrival here but at heart, he's a good boy."

"Boshengro – is that his name?" Neil asked.

"No, no – his name is Rick. *Boshengro* means the man with the fiddle. We call him that, because that is what he is." She had been smiling, but now her face darkened, as if she had something more on her mind. "Nothing means more to Rick than his violin."

*

Neil and the others returned to their own camp very late. Emily and Julie couldn't stop yawning. Kate packed them off into the camper van, said goodnight, then followed them soon after.

"I don't feel sleepy," Neil said. "Max, how about taking the dogs along the shore? They haven't had a proper run all day."

Max agreed, and whistled for Prince.

"Is that OK, Glen?" Neil asked.

"It's pretty late," said Glen, "but sure, if you want to. Don't be too long, though, and make sure the dogs stay with you."

Neil and Max, with Sam and Prince trotting at heel, set off along the footpath beside the lake, away from the gypsy camp. When they reached a more open section of the shore, with shingle stretching down to the water's edge, Neil stopped and found a stick to throw for the dogs.

They raced across the shingle, barking excitedly. Sam was just ahead, Prince following with ears streaming out behind. Sam snapped up the stick and veered back towards his owner.

"Bad luck, Prince!" Max called, and threw a second stick. "Here!"

When both dogs had run off their surplus

energy, and gone to snuffle after something at the water's edge, Neil and Max started to stroll back.

Max had started telling Neil more about the *Time Travellers* film, and then stopped as Neil reached out and grabbed his arm. "What's the matter?"

"I thought I heard something."

Just ahead a clump of undergrowth straggled almost to the water's edge, cutting off the next stretch of the lakeshore. Treading softly, Neil and Max approached. Neil heard the noise again, the sound of a bow being drawn across violin strings, a single note. He glanced at Max, who nodded.

Parting the bushes, they saw Rick, the gypsy violinist, standing alone by the lake. He played another note, turned one of the tuning pegs a fraction, and then positioned the instrument under his chin. A cascade of notes showered out into the night air.

"Why's he playing by himself?" Neil asked in a low murmur. "He's nowhere near the camp."

Max was frowning slightly as he listened.

Just then Prince trotted up inquisitively, closely followed by Sam. Max said softly, "Quiet!" and the well-trained Prince settled down at once. Neil put a hand over Sam's muzzle. The Border collie sat, head cocked alertly as if he was listening to the violin too.

As Rick played on, Neil realized that this was nothing like the wild gypsy music he had played in the camp. This was complicated, precise, and though Neil was no musician, he would have betted it was a lot more difficult to play.

"He's *really* good," Max whispered.

For a few minutes more they stood watching the tall, slender figure outlined against the silvery waters of the lake and listened to the melody of the violin. Then Neil motioned Max away. The dogs padding silently at heel as the two boys skirted the gypsy dreamer.

When he thought they were out of earshot, Neil said, "That was weird!"

"You don't know how weird," Max began. "My mum's really into classical music and I'm sure she's got that piece on CD. I mean, you can't play that kind of thing unless you're really good!" He stood still, and watched the two dogs as they trotted ahead, tails waving. "I just wonder," he went on, "where a gypsy would learn to play like that. And why he's playing on his own where no one will hear him?"

Chapter Six

Sunlight dappled the surface of the lake as Neil emerged, gasping, and stood chest deep, with water streaming off his hair and down his face. "It's freezing!" he yelled.

It was the following morning. Max and Julie had gone with Kate to visit Ainsworth Castle; Max had left Neil in charge of Prince, in case dogs weren't allowed inside.

Sam dog-paddled around him enthusiastically.

"It's all right for you," said Neil. "You've got hair all over." He was convinced Sam was grinning at him. Neil launched himself forward and swam a few strokes inshore to where Emily

59

was paddling and stooping to pick things out of the water.

"What are you doing?" he asked.

"Looking for stones." His sister showed him a handful. "If you can find the right ones you can polish them up and make great paperweights."

Prince came dashing along the water's edge, splashing and barking. Sam joined in and shook himself vigorously, then the two dogs charged off into the bushes.

"I'd better get them dry," Neil said, wading out to the nearby heap of towels. "Here, Sam, Prince!"

He vigorously towelled Sam dry, while Emily did the same for Prince. Sam was panting, but he looked bright-eyed and eager.

Neil dried himself and went back to the tent to get dressed. Glen, who was lying on the grass reading a book, tossed him a tube of suncream. Neil smeared it over his bare arms and neck, and with a sudden idea, bent down and put a dab on the dogs' noses.

"What on earth are you doing?" Emily asked, laughing as Sam and Prince drew their heads back.

Neil wondered what the stuff smelt like to a

dog. "I reckon if it's skin, it can get sunburnt," he said, making a mental note to buy some more cream and add it to his dog emergency kit.

Later that morning Neil decided that the time had come to do something about King. Ever since he'd seen the Great Dane's eyes, he had been worrying. Nothing bothered Neil more than the idea of a dog in pain. If Lord Ainsworth didn't care that King was suffering, then someone would have to make him.

"And I guess that's me," Neil muttered to himself. He was walking with Sam along the lakeshore in the direction of Ainsworth Castle while Kate was settling in properly at the new campsite. Glen had taken Max and Prince in the van to the village so Max could phone the *Time Travellers* director, Brian Mason. Neil had left Emily and Julie at the gypsy camp, visiting Keziah and Chavi.

He had just passed the place where they had camped on their first night when he heard movement in the shrubbery ahead. Sam, who had been weaving back and forth, sniffing at all the exciting hollows among the tree roots, stopped and cocked an ear. Neil halted and slapped his leg to bring Sam back to his side as first King, then Penny, appeared round a turn in the path.

Penny also halted abruptly and said, "Oh, it's you again."

Neil thought she was giving him the sort of look she would give to a slug in her salad. The Great Dane stood beside her, head up, on guard, until Penny said, "All right, King." Then he paced across the clearing, nosed Neil in a friendly way and dipped his head to sniff at Sam. Sam, who was used to meeting lots of strange dogs at King Street, gave him a friendly sniff in return.

"Hi, King," Neil said. "Hi, Penny." He took out a dog treat, and while King ate it he had another look at his eyes. They were watering again, and some of the fluid had dried and crusted around King's eyelids. The eyes themselves looked inflamed. Neil suddenly felt furious. Couldn't the Ainsworths see what was wrong with this great dog? Didn't they care? "Come and look at this," he said to Penny.

She crossed the clearing and joined Neil and the dogs.

"See," Neil said, laying his hands one on either side of King's head and tilting it so Penny had to look at the eyes. "Can't you see his eyes are hurting?"

Penny suddenly looked as if she was going to cry. "I know. But what can I do?"

"You can get your dad to do something!"

"No, I—" She clamped her lips together. For a minute Neil thought she might scream, or even hit him. Then she lowered her head, and stroked King's ears. The huge Great Dane leant into her touch with a blissful expression. It was obvious that Penny really loved the huge dog.

"Money is the problem," she explained. "It's not that my dad doesn't *care* about King. But he's afraid that he might need an expensive operation, and if he couldn't afford it the vet might tell him to have King put down."

Neil could hardly speak for a minute. "But he's Lord Ainsworth! He's got the castle and all this land. He *can't* be short of money!"

Penny gave a short, unhappy laugh. "You've no idea." She sat down on a log; King came to sit beside her, pushing his head up against her, and she put an arm round him.

Neil squatted down opposite Penny.

"You see, Neil, it takes a lot of money to run the castle. Just keeping it in good repair costs the earth. We need some work done on the roof, but Adrian says we can't afford it this year. The income from renting the land doesn't nearly cover everything."

"But what about the visitors – people pay to go in, don't they?"

Penny smiled, as if she was starting to thaw. "That was Adrian's idea. We only started it last year. My dad hates it. Only a very few people know about Ainsworth Castle yet. It all helps, but it's still not enough."

She hugged King, and the Great Dane rested his noble head against her shoulder. "There just isn't any money for enormous vets' bills."

"Then *you* should get some," Neil said.

"But I can't—" Penny broke off again, frowning, but not unfriendly this time, just thoughtful. "Do you think I could earn some money? Myself?"

Neil shrugged. "Run errands, maybe. Walk other people's dogs."

Penny had brightened, and then shook her head. "Neil, I can't! My dad would have a fit. Lord Ainsworth's daughter getting paid for dog-walking!"

Neil grinned. He was beginning to feel much better. Penny was treating him like a human being now, and an ally in making a plan to help King.

"You seem to know what's wrong with him," she said. "Do you know how much it would cost to put it right?"

Neil shook his head. "It probably *will* be expensive." He wanted to say that nobody could put a price on King's sight, but he realized the problem wasn't as simple as that. If Lord Ainsworth really didn't have the money then it would have to come from somewhere else. "Do you know your vet well?" he asked. "Would he tell you how much it would cost – without charging you?"

"Oh, yes, he's really nice," Penny said. "He's called David Blackburn. He lives here in Beckthwaite."

Neil sprang to his feet. "So what are we waiting for? Let's go and ask him!"

Penny stared up at him. "But what will my dad say?"

"Your dad doesn't have to find out, does he?" Neil suggested. "Not until we've made some sort of plan, anyway."

He waited impatiently while Penny thought this over. At last she got to her feet. "Well . . . all right."

"Great!" Neil took her arm and hustled her up the track to the road. The two dogs followed side by side. Penny still looked worried, but Neil wasn't going to let her escape now.

When they reached the road, they turned in the direction of Beckthwaite, but before they had gone more than a few yards Neil saw the white camper van driving towards them. It pulled up beside them and Glen leant out of the window.

"Hi, Neil. Do you want a lift back?"

"No, thanks. Glen, this is Penny."

"Hi." Glen smiled at Penny, who smiled shyly back at him. "Lord Ainsworth's daughter, yes? Neil told me all about you."

There was a sudden eruption from inside the van as Max scrambled out with Prince at his heels. "Neil, I've got great news – hi, Penny – I phoned Brian and—"

"I'll get on," Glen interrupted, grinning. "Back at the site for lunch, OK."

"Sure," said Neil. "Max, calm down. Tell us properly."

Max was fizzing with excitement, but he waited for the camper van to drive off before he continued. "I phoned Brian Mason. He's really worried about finding a castle for *The Time*

66

Travellers. Everywhere's in ruins, or has modern bits built on, or the owners won't let him film. So when I told him about Ainsworth Castle he said he'd phone Adrian Bartlett right away and make an appointment to come and see it." He beamed at Penny. "What about that?"

Penny's eyes were sparkling. "Max, that's wonderful! I hope my dad agrees."

"You'll have to make him," said Neil.

Penny sighed. "Nobody *makes* Daddy do anything."

"But look – Max, the film company will pay quite a lot for using the castle, won't they?"

Max shrugged. "It depends what you mean by quite a lot."

"Enough for King to have his eyes fixed and fix a few leaky roofs?"

"Oh, yes." Max beamed again. "Easily enough for that."

"There you are, then," Neil said to Penny. "All you have to do is to persuade your dad to let them film at the castle, and then use the money to pay for King's operation."

Penny put a hand to her head, and brushed back her long, fair hair. "All I have to do!"

"But he must want King to be—" Neil broke

off at the sound of loud barking from somewhere behind him. He looked round, but both
Sam and Prince were sitting quietly by the side
of the road. Then he saw where King was. He'd
wandered about fifty metres further on and
stood in the middle of the road with his head
cocked as if he too was listening to the barking.

"King!" Penny called. "King, come here!"

A car appeared round a bend in the road
from the direction of the village. King was facing
the vehicle, staring right at it, but he didn't
move.

"King!" Penny shouted again, starting to run
towards him, but the Great Dane was too far
away to reach.

The car bore down on the dog and there was
nothing Neil or the others could do.

Chapter Seven

The car's horn sounded. It was a red sporty model and approaching very fast.

King cocked his head as if he'd heard the horn but nevertheless seemed rooted to the spot, unable to move. Suddenly, as it seemed almost too late to save him, the loud barking began again and a silver shape streaked out of the bushes beside the road. It was Chavi. She hurled herself at King and struck him in the flank, nudging him sideways. The Great Dane started, then sprang onto the verge out of the path of the car with Chavi by his side.

The sports car swerved slightly and snarled past, horn still blaring. Neil caught a glimpse of the driver, a young man, shouting something furiously before he vanished around the next bend.

"Maniac!" said Max.

Neil checked that the road was clear before running across it to where King and Chavi were on the opposite verge. The Weimaraner stood shaking herself.

Penny flung herself down on her knees beside the Great Dane. "King! Are you hurt, boy?" She sobbed and ran her hands over the dog's back and limbs, trying to check whether he was hurt or not. She was crying too much to be able to see properly. "King, I thought that car was going to kill you!"

"Calm down," Neil said, patting her shoulder. "I think he's OK. Let me look."

The Great Dane was already standing again. Neil examined him carefully. He couldn't see any visible sign of injury, and King didn't flinch from his touch. At first he was shivering as if he was in shock, but gradually, as Penny patted and soothed him, the shivering died away.

"That's better, boy," he said. "You're just fine. Look, Penny, he's not hurt."

Penny was sniffing and trying to smile. Neil thought she looked more shocked than her dog.

"I think King's going to be fine," insisted Neil. "But Penny, you know why it happened, don't you?"

Penny nodded. "He couldn't see the car." Her voice trembled a little. "And because of that, he didn't understand why we were shouting!"

"This means you have to get him to a vet right away. He might have been killed, if it wasn't for Chavi." He turned to the Weimaraner, who had come up to investigate, as if she wanted to be sure she had acted in time. "You're a clever girl, aren't you?" he said. Then he frowned as something struck him. "Yes, you are clever . . . There's something weird going on here!"

"What?" asked Max.

71

"Chavi started barking *before* she saw the car." Neil was shocked. "Even before the car came round the bend. It's almost as if she was trying to get our attention, to warn us about it."

"That's ridiculous," Max said. "I mean, she couldn't have known King was in danger.

Max and Penny both stared at the Weimaraner. "The barking made us look up," said Penny. "But she must have heard the car . . . or something."

Neil realized that Penny had never been to the gypsy camp, or heard Keziah's stories about how Chavi could foretell the future. He couldn't quite believe that the beautiful Weimaraner was *psychic.* But there was certainly something odd about her. If nothing else, she was unbelievably brave.

He had just started to explain Keziah's stories to Penny when a voice called, "Neil! Neil!" and he saw Emily and Julie appear from the trees on the other side of the road.

"So you've got her!" Emily said as she and Julie joined the others. She stroked Chavi's head. "She just started barking her head off and took off through the trees like a rocket. I thought we'd lost her. What were you playing at, you bad girl?"

72

"She saved King's life," said Penny.

Emily stared as Neil explained what had happened. "You're fantastic!" she told Chavi, kneeling beside the Weimaraner and giving her a hug. "You deserve a medal!"

"Now do you believe Keziah's stories?" Julie asked.

"I don't know what to believe," Neil replied.

"Huh!" said his sister.

While Emily went on petting the Weimaraner, Max finished explaining to Penny about the gypsy dog's prophetic powers.

"That's incredible!" said Penny.

"You should tell your dad," Neil suggested. "He might be a bit more friendly to the gypsies. King would be dead now if it wasn't for Chavi."

Penny shuddered. "Don't!"

"And Lord Ainsworth would have no heir," Emily added. "And Ainsworth Castle would fall into the lake. Isn't that what the legend says, if the line of Great Danes dies out?"

Penny pressed her face into the Great Dane's flank. King bent his head and nosed her hair as if he was trying to comfort her. He was such a loving and gentle dog, Neil thought, in spite of his huge size and strength.

"It's OK, Penny, it didn't happen," said Max.

Penny looked up. "I've always felt safe with King. Daddy lets me go anywhere, as long as King is with me. He's my very best friend. I don't know what I'd do without him."

Emily went to her and put an arm round her shoulders. "It'll be all right. You'll see."

Penny gave her a watery smile.

"All the same," Neil said, "this just shows that you've got to get King's eyes seen to. Are we going to see your vet now?"

Penny scrambled to her feet and looked down at herself. Her jeans were torn and streaked with grass-stains where she had flung herself down beside King. "I don't think I'd better," she said.

Neil was about to protest when he realized that Penny's face was streaked with tears, her eyes were still red and her hair was all over the place. "You might give him a shock," he admitted. "Why don't you get cleaned up, and I'll meet you after lunch and go with you?"

Penny shook her head. "I can't this afternoon. I promised Adrian I'd help with the visitors."

Neil hoped she wasn't having second thoughts. He was determined to get King to the vet if it was the last thing he ever did. "When can you, then?" he asked.

"Tomorrow," Penny said. "I'll meet you in the clearing where we met this morning. Same time. I usually walk King around then."

"All right," Neil said, grinning. "And if you don't turn up, I'll come and fetch you!"

Penny looked as if she wasn't sure whether he was joking. "I'll be there," she said. "I promise."

Neil and the others watched Penny as she led King down the road towards the turning to Ainsworth Castle. When she was out of sight they called the dogs to heel.

"We'd better take Chavi home," Emily said, as they set off. "I don't know what I'd have told Keziah if she'd gone missing."

"Well, we've got a good story to tell her now," said Julie. "All about how she saved King."

"Anyway," Neil added, "I think Chavi only goes missing when *she* wants to. Look at the way she found us."

Emily frowned thoughtfully. "Yes," she said. "We still haven't worked that out. Maybe she had a reason for taking us down to Ainsworth Castle?"

"So Max can make a good film?" Neil guessed, grinning.

Emily swiped at him. "No, something more serious than that!"

"Maybe she wanted us to meet Penny?" Max suggested.

"So we can help King?" That seemed a very good reason to Neil.

"But Lord Ainsworth has to agree about the film and King's operation," Julie pointed out. "It's all for nothing if he won't."

"Penny will persuade him," Neil said, but he wasn't sure that was true. Lord Ainsworth wasn't the sort of man who changed his mind easily. He patted the Weimaraner, who was loping along beside him. "Come on, girl," he said, only half joking. "Show us how to sort out Lord Ainsworth!"

The Weimaraner raised her head and gave him a look as if she had understood what he was asking and was thinking how best to go about it. *You give it your best shot, girl*, Neil thought, *because I don't know what to do.*

On their way down the lane to the campsite, Chavi suddenly stopped, head raised.

"What's the matter, girl?" Neil asked. "Get a move on. I want my lunch!"

For all his urging, the Weimaraner would not move.

"Leave her, Neil," Emily said. "Let's see what she wants. It might be important."

Neil stood still and waited.

Everyone was quiet.

Then Neil heard movement in the woodland to their right.

"Someone's there," said Julie.

Before Neil had time to wonder what Chavi had in her head this time, she gave a welcoming bark as Rick the violinist stepped out onto the path with a bundle of wood on his shoulder. He shifted the bundle so he could support it with

one arm and scratch the dog's ears.

"Hi there, Chavi." Noticing Neil and the others he added, "Hello."

He sounded stiff – not welcoming or friendly. Neil thought his voice sounded different from the rest of the gypsies.

"We heard you playing last night," Emily said. "You were brilliant."

Rick gave her a cool nod. "Thank you."

"Are you going back to the camp?" Neil asked. "Can we help you carry the wood?"

"No thanks, I can manage." Rick still sounded cool, but he fell into step with them as they went on down the lane.

"Chavi's great," Emily said to him. "She just saved King from being run over."

Rick paused, looking down at her. "What?"

"Do you know King?" Neil asked. "The Great Dane from Ainsworth Castle. He couldn't see a car coming, and Chavi pushed him out of the way just in time. She was really brave."

"Why couldn't King see the car?" Rick asked.

"There's something wrong with his eyes," Neil explained.

"What?"

Rick's interrogation seemed very odd to Neil, but there was no reason not to answer. "It's his eyelids. They're turning inwards and irritating his eyes. He needs an operation."

Rick's brows snapped together in a fierce frown, and Neil had a feeling that there was something familiar about him. "So why can't he have one?"

"I don't really know," said Neil, "but I think it's because Lord Ainsworth can't afford it."

Rick exploded. "Hah!" He strode on more quickly. Behind him, Neil and the others exchanged glances, and Max tapped his forehead. Brilliant musician or not, Neil thought, Rick was *very* peculiar.

As they reached the edge of the campsite, Chavi pressed up against Rick, and seized his shirtsleeve very gently between her teeth. Rick looked down, frowning, and tried to shake free, but Chavi held on. "What are you doing? Let go!"

Chavi just tugged gently at his sleeve.

"Maybe she's trying to tell you something," Julie suggested.

Chavi tugged again at Rick's sleeve, resisting the violinist's attempts to free himself.

"I think she wants you to follow her," Neil said.

With a bewildered look, Rick set the bundle of wood down, and followed the Weimaraner a few paces through the edge of the trees. The dog was heading for the lakeshore footpath.

"What's she up to now?" Neil said. "There's nothing down there but Ainsworth Castle."

Rick stopped dead. The Weimaraner dug her feet into the ground and gave him a more determined pull, but this time he refused to move.

Max laughed. "She knows the future," he said. "You should go with her."

"Find out what fate has in store," Neil added.

Rick ignored both of them. He shook his arm savagely, pulling away so that Chavi's front feet were lifted off the ground. "Get off!" he said furiously.

His shirt tore. Chavi dropped onto all fours with a scrap of checked material in her mouth, while Rick drew away, white with anger, flapping the torn sleeve. "Leave me alone, you stupid mutt!" he shouted.

Turning, he scooped up the bundle of wood and almost ran back through the trees towards the campsite. Chavi looked after him mournfully.

"That was really weird!" Julie breathed out.

"Yes," Emily agreed. "Why should Chavi want to take Rick to Ainsworth Castle?"

"And not only that," said Neil. "Why didn't he want to go?"

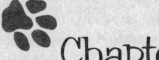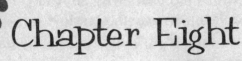

Chapter Eight

David Blackburn, the local vet, straightened up from examining King's eyes. He was a stocky young man with short fair hair and big, capable hands.

"Do you know what's the matter with King?" Penny asked anxiously. "Can you do anything about it?"

"Yes, and yes," the vet replied. "It's a good thing you brought him in."

"Neil said I should," Penny said.

It was the day after King's accident, and they were all in David Blackburn's examination room in Beckthwaite. King had sat patiently while the vet had a good look at his eyes, as if he knew that help was on its way.

"You certainly know dogs, Neil," the vet said.

Neil felt himself going red at the vet's praise. "My mum and dad run a boarding kennels," he explained. "I've grown up with dogs. I think they're just great."

The vet gave him a broad smile. "I won't argue with that. And your own dog's a splendid chap."

Sam, who had watched the examination with great interest, thumped his tail on the floor a couple of times.

"You see," the vet went on to Penny, "as Neil suspected, King's eyelids are slowly turning inwards, so his eyelashes scratch the surface of his eye. It's called entropion. If it's not treated, I'm afraid he'll go blind. The good news is that with the operation he'll be completely cured."

Penny smiled. "That's wonderful!" Her smile faded. "But I suppose it'll be really expensive?"

"It won't be cheap, I'm afraid." Mr Blackburn hesitated and said slowly, "Look, Penny, I know your dad can be difficult. But he's got to decide. This dog is in serious discomfort, and in danger of going blind. I'll tell you what. Why don't I give Lord Ainsworth a ring and tell him – what the

danger is, how much it's going to cost, everything. How does that sound?"

"Great!" said Neil.

Penny smiled and nodded. "Oh, thank you.
My dad would be furious if I told him."

"Well, he doesn't frighten me," said the vet.
"Besides . . . he does care for King, I'm sure he
docs." He patted King and rumpled his ears.
"Don't you worry, old chap. You're going to be
just fine." He made some notes on a record
card, and added to Penny, "There's something
else you should think about – it's not a problem
now, but it might be later."

"What?" Penny asked apprehensively.

"This legend of yours – that Ainsworth Castle will fall if the line of Great Danes fails. I get the feeling your dad takes it seriously. Well, entropion can be an inherited disease. I wouldn't advise you to breed from King."

"But that means the line *will* end when King dies!" Penny went over to King and put an arm across his back as if she thought he was going to drop dead on the spot.

"No," Neil and David said together, and then grinned at each other. David waved a hand at Neil, giving him the chance to explain.

"All you need to do is get a pup from a different part of King's bloodline." When Penny still looked blank, Neil added, "King's cousin, say. So that they have the same ancestors."

"Oh, I see!" Penny said, relieved. "That's all right." She looked down at King and caressed him; the huge dog gave her a trustful look with his damaged eyes. "But I hope we won't have to think about that for ages yet."

David went across the examination room to wash his hands. "That's settled, then. When would be a good time to ring your father?"

"Sometime this evening," Penny replied. He's always in a better mood then. Oh . . ." She turned to Neil. "I know you think he's awful.

But he can be kind . . . and fun. It's just that he's got a lot of worries."

"Sure," Neil said, grinning.

He got the impression that Penny had been about to say something else, and at the last minute had decided not to. He couldn't help feeling that money wasn't the only thing that worried Lord Ainsworth.

Neil and Penny led their dogs out of the surgery and back through the village. Penny was keeping King on a lead now, to be sure he didn't step out in front of any more cars.

She walked along the road with Neil as far as the turning down to the gypsy camp, where they said goodbye.

"Let's meet again tomorrow," Neil suggested. "Same time, same place. Then you can tell me what your dad says when David phones him."

"Yes, all right." Penny went pink, hesitated, and then added, "I'm really grateful to you, Neil. If King gets well, it'll all be because of you."

"Oh, I don't—" Neil was beginning, when the noise of breaking twigs told him that someone was walking in the woods just behind him. He turned.

At the same moment King stiffened, and let

out a deep-toned bark. Rick stepped out into the lane.

Just like the dog, he stiffened, and seemed as if he would retreat into the trees. Penny's voice stopped him; to Neil's astonishment she exclaimed, "Richie!"

Instead of standing to guard Penny, as Neil would have expected, King pulled towards Rick as far as his lead would let him go. Penny dropped the loop, and the Great Dane sprang forward, reared up and put his paws on Rick's shoulders, while his tongue swiped over his face.

Rick staggered back, recovered, and reached out to rub the great dog's ears. "Hey, King, steady on," he murmured. "Down, boy. It's OK. Down."

King dropped to all fours, and Rick bent down and ruffled his fur.

Penny said, "What are you doing here?"

Rick turned his gaze on her, and his face hardened.

Neil thought they had forgotten him. They were staring at each other, and Penny was looking furious.

"I'm with the gypsies," Rick said. "I go where they go."

Penny glared at him. "Of all the stupid—"

"Stupid!" Rick was shouting now. "Who are you calling stupid? What else am I supposed to do?"

"Not this!" Penny had gone scarlet, and Neil thought she was going to burst into tears. "You're spoiling everything!"

"*I'm* spoiling everything? That's a good one!"

"You've got to come and talk to Daddy."

"Talk!" Rick exploded. "I said that I'd never set foot on Ainsworth land again and I meant it. If he wants to talk to me he can come to the camp."

"You know he won't do that." Penny's tears were spilling over now.

"Then he's a stubborn old idiot. Besides, we haven't got anything to say to each other. I know he's never going to change his mind, and I'm certainly not going to change mine."

"You're as bad as he is!" Penny sobbed. "You don't care! You don't even care about King!"

Rick took a step forward; he had gone white. "That's not true."

"Then why are you doing this? You and Daddy? I hate both of you!"

She groped for the end of King's lead, grabbed it and tried to pull him away. King

hung back. Rick said, more quietly, "Go on, boy. Go with Penny."

Reluctantly, the Great Dane obeyed him, and Penny was able to turn away and lead him back along the road. Neil called after her, "Don't forget tomorrow!" but she was still crying, and Neil didn't think she'd heard him.

"Well, how about that?" he said to Sam. Sam cocked his head as if he was just as mystified as Neil.

Neil turned back to Rick. The violinist was stalking straight-backed down the lane towards the camp.

"Hey, Rick!" he called. "Wait for me!"

He wanted to ask why Penny was so upset, but Rick didn't wait, and as Neil dashed after him he guessed that Rick was unlikely to tell him anyway.

The violinist was almost running by the time he reached the camp. Neil caught him up as he stormed out into the clearing and collided with one of the gypsy boys who was taking a load of wood to the fire.

The wood scattered everywhere. The boy pushed Rick angrily. "Stupid *gaujo*! Now see what you've done."

Rick clenched his fists and looked as if he was going to hit the boy. Keziah, who was stirring the cooking pot over the fire, looked up and called out, "Rick! Nat! No fighting in the camp!"

The boy, Nat, hissed something between his teeth. Rick did not reply. His shoulders sagged and he started to pick up the fallen wood. After a minute, Nat helped him, and they took the branches over to the fire together.

Keziah spoke to Rick, who seemed to be explaining something to her at length, but they were too far away for Neil to hear. He looked around. There was the usual quiet activity in the camp. Near Keziah's *vardo* he saw Emily with Chavi, and strolled over to her.

"What was all that about?" Emily asked.

"Don't ask me." Neil squatted down and fished out a dog treat for Chavi, and then for Sam, who came nosing up for his share. "It was really weird. Rick and Penny met at the top of the lane, and they just went for each other. Penny was crying."

"That's awful!" said Emily, immediately sympathetic. "Is she OK?"

Neil shrugged. "I don't know. She went home with King. I'm seeing her again tomorrow."

"I'll come with you," said Emily. She went on petting Chavi and asked, "Do you know what she was upset about? Had Rick done something?"

"No, that's what's so weird. The minute they set eyes on each other they started yelling at each other. They've obviously met before."

"They can't have! Lord Ainsworth wouldn't let his precious daughter go anywhere near the gypsies!"

"Maybe Lord Ainsworth doesn't know," Neil guessed. "And I'll tell you something else. King guards Penny, but he didn't guard her from Rick. He jumped up and started licking his face."

Emily giggled. "That must have been worth seeing."

"King must have recognized his scent. And he wanted to stay with Rick instead of going with Penny. Rick had to send him away, but I don't think he wanted to."

"Likes the dog, can't stand Penny," Emily said. "You're right, Neil, it is weird."

"And then he comes back here in such a temper that he nearly starts a fight with Nat. Nat called him a stupid – what was the word – a stupid *gaujo*."

"He called him *what*?" Emily suddenly sat up straight.

"A stupid *gaujo*."

Emily squirmed excitedly. "Neil, listen. Keziah's teaching me to *rokra Romani* – that means to speak the Romany language. And *gaujo* is the word for anyone who's not a gypsy."

"What? Are you telling me that Rick isn't a gypsy?"

"If that's what Nat said."

"Well, if that's right," Neil said, frowning, "then who on earth is he?"

Chapter Nine

"She's late," said Neil.

He glanced at his watch. Along with Emily and Sam, he was waiting in the clearing where Penny usually came with King. She was already half an hour late.

"Maybe her dad won't let her come," Emily said.

"Her dad doesn't know she's been meeting me."

"Neil, you can't be sure about that," Emily pointed out. "Not after yesterday. If Penny told Lord Ainsworth about Rick, and if the vet phoned about King's operation – well, we just don't know what he would do." She frowned worriedly. "She might be in trouble."

Neil glanced at his watch again, and wandered a few paces down the footpath towards the castle. Still no Penny. "Right," he said. "I've had enough. I'm going to the castle to find out what's going on." He turned back to face Emily. "Are you coming?"

Emily was already following. "What do you think?"

The sun was shining when they came out of the trees into the clear space at the end of the castle causeway. As before, visitors were strolling in and out of the gate.

Neil strode determinedly across the causeway, with Sam trotting at heel.

"There's a notice that says all dogs have to be on leads," Emily said. "And we might have to pay to get in."

"I don't see why," said Neil. "We don't want to tour the place. We just want to speak to Penny."

All the same, he took Sam's lead from his pocket and bent down to clip it on, slipping a dog treat to the Border collie at the same time. "I know you don't need it, Sam," he said, "but we've got to stick to the rules. No point in making Lord Ainsworth angry for nothing."

With Sam on the lead and Emily beside him,

he stepped underneath the archway and into the castle.

They stood in a large paved courtyard. Opposite was a flight of stone steps leading to a massive oak doorway with iron hinges and studs. A large black cat was sunning itself on the balustrade, and Adrian Bartlett stood stroking it.

"Cats!" Neil muttered.

Still, he was relieved to see someone he knew; Mr Bartlett had been friendly the last time they met. He crossed the courtyard. "Hello."

Adrian Bartlett looked up from the cat, which gave Sam a baleful stare but did not move from its place in the sun. "Oh, hello." He gave them both a vague smile. "What can I do for you?"

"We've come to see Penny," said Neil, and added belatedly, "Please."

"I'm not sure you can . . . No," Mr Bartlett said as Neil opened his mouth to protest. "I haven't locked her up in the dungeons. It's just that I haven't seen her about. She usually walks King around this time," he explained.

Neil felt a sinking in his stomach. If Penny had taken King out, but not come to the meeting place, that must mean she didn't want to talk to him. "Is she all right?" he asked.

"As far as I know," Adrian Bartlett replied, looking surprised. "Shouldn't she be?"

"We don't know," said Emily. "It's just that she was upset when she met Rick yesterday."

Mr Bartlett stiffened. His hand was motionless on the cat's head. He peered at Emily through his gold-rimmed glasses and said quietly, "Met who?"

"Rick," said Neil. "Although Penny called him Richie. He lives with the gypsies."

Adrian Bartlett was silent. Neil had the impression of frantic thinking going on underneath his calm exterior.

Eventually he asked, "Does Lord Ainsworth know about this, Neil?"

Neil shrugged. "I've no idea."

For a minute longer Mr Bartlett went on thinking, and then shook his head slightly and smiled. "I had a phone call yesterday," he said. "From . . . Brian Mason, I think his name was. He's from the *Time Travellers* production company. He should be here later today to have a look at the castle."

This was great news. Neil almost failed to notice that Mr Bartlett had deliberately changed the subject.

"I'm sure he'll like it," Mr Bartlett went on

enthusiastically. "Can't you just see King Arthur and Queen Guinevere coming down these steps? With all—"

"I'd rather see Penny," Neil interrupted.

"Please," Emily said earnestly. "We only want to help. Do you have any idea why Rick upset her?"

Mr Bartlett pushed his glasses back up his nose. "I'm sorry," he said. "I can't talk about this. It's complicated, and – well, I know you're trying to help, but none of us set eyes on you before this week. I'm afraid I can't start telling you Lord Ainsworth's private business."

That was fair enough, Neil thought sadly. None of this was anything to do with them. All he had wanted to begin with was to help King.

"OK," Neil said, trying to control his curiosity. "Will you tell Penny we called to see her, please?"

"Yes, I will," Mr Bartlett replied.

As they walked away, he saw a very worried expression on the steward's face. He suddenly felt determined to find out the truth about Rick – and how he knew Penny and King.

Neil and Emily returned to the camp just in time to set off with everyone for a walk into the

97

surrounding hills. They climbed a steep track beside a waterfall, as far as the gravelly path overlooking the lake below. The rooftops of Beckthwaite village were just visible among the trees, and beyond that the grey walls of Ainsworth Castle, looking like a toy fort.

When they reached a grassy area, Max flopped down where the ground levelled out a bit. "This would do for the picnic," he said. "Is it time for lunch?"

Everyone sat down and Kate shared out cheese and salad rolls and cans of drink. Neil took the dogs' bowls from his backpack and poured water for Sam and Prince. He watched the dogs nosing around among the gorse and heather further up the slope. The day was warm and still.

Suddenly the peace was shattered by a squeal from Prince. The cocker spaniel came skidding down the hill, yelping furiously. Sam followed, but he was quiet; whatever was bothering Prince had not affected him.

"Prince!" Max sprang up, scattering food, and dashed over to his dog. "Prince, what's the matter?"

Prince pulled away from his hands. He was whimpering and pawing at his mouth with one foot. Max glanced helplessly at Neil, who had already come to join him. "Neil, he's hurt. What is it?"

Neil tried to examine Prince, but the distressed dog wouldn't keep still. "Can you calm him down?" he said to Max. "We can't have a proper look while he's dancing about like that."

Kate came over, while Emily and Julie and Glen looked on anxiously. Emily gripped Sam's collar to keep him out of the way. "He might have stood on a thorn," she said.

Max grabbed Prince and hugged him, speaking soothingly, and gradually the cocker spaniel grew quieter, though he still kept up the unhappy whining.

"No, it's a bee sting; look," said Kate. She pointed to a soft swelling on the side of Prince's mouth. "Neil, it's time for that dog emergency kit of yours."

Neil was already rooting around inside the plastic box. He brought out a pair of tweezers and gave them to Kate. She bent close to Prince's mouth, and plucked away something too tiny for Neil to see from where he was. "Got it," she said with satisfaction.

Neil was squeezing something from a plastic bottle onto a pad of cotton wool.

"What's that?" Max asked. He had gone white; Neil knew how much he cared for Prince.

"Bicarbonate of soda in water," Neil said. "Here, you bathe him with it." He passed the soaked pad over to Max, who dabbed it gently against the swelling on Prince's mouth. Prince was already growing quieter, though he was trembling and panting rapidly.

"Will he be all right?" Max asked.

"Sure he will," said Kate. "But if he still looks unhappy when we get back, we'll drop in on the vet."

Max looked up at Neil with a weak smile. "I'm

really glad you had your kit with you."

Neil grinned smugly. "All part of the Puppy Patrol service, mate."

That evening, Prince had recovered and was trotting along happily by the time the group reached Beckthwaite again.

When they came into the village square, they saw a small group of about ten people huddled around the market cross. Among them Neil recognized Adrian Bartlett, looking even more worried than he had that morning.

Neil went up to him. "Is anything the matter?"

Before Mr Bartlett could reply, Lord Ainsworth came out of the Ainsworth Arms and strode across to them. "They haven't seen her either," he said.

Catching sight of Neil, he stood over him with eyebrows and moustache bristling. "You, boy. Have you seen my daughter?"

"Penny's missing," Adrian Bartlett explained. "No one has seen her all day."

"Well, we haven't, either," Neil said.

"We've been up in the hills," Kate added, coming over to see what was going on.

"We'll help you look," Emily offered.

"Or maybe King could help you find her," Neil suggested.

"King's gone too," said Mr Bartlett. "They must be together somewhere – but we don't know where."

Lord Ainsworth snorted through his moustache. "We've turned the castle upside down. No one's seen her. We'll have to try the police. Come on, Adrian." As he strode away he glanced back and added, "Thank you."

Neil was even more startled. He had stopped expecting Lord Ainsworth to be polite. But he hadn't sounded rude or angry this time, just worried because his daughter was missing. Just like Dad would be if it was him or Emily, Neil thought.

"We'll look anyway!" Neil called after him, though he was not sure Lord Ainsworth heard.

The villagers around the market cross talked among themselves. Neil caught one or two hostile glances, as if some of them at least still thought they were with the gypsies. He tried to ignore them as Emily clutched his arm.

"Penny didn't meet us this morning," Emily said. "She could have disappeared any time."

"Maybe someone kidnapped her," suggested Julie. "For a ransom. Her father is a lord."

102

"A lord without any money," Neil reminded her. "Besides, King's with her. King wouldn't let anyone lay a finger on Penny. She must have gone of her own accord."

"But where?" Julie asked.

"If she was upset about seeing Rick," Max said thoughtfully, "do you think she might have gone to see him again?"

"The way she behaved, I think Rick's the last person she would want to see," Neil replied.

"But she might have gone to the gypsy camp," Emily suggested. "I bet Lord Ainsworth never thought to look there!"

One of the villagers turned round as Emily spoke, and grabbed her shoulder. It was the landlord of the Ainsworth Arms. "What's that, lass? You think Penny's with the gypsies?"

Emily looked scared, and took a step back.

"Steady on," said Glen.

"Penny was talking to one of them, that's all," Neil said.

The man stared hard at them for a minute and then turned back to his friends. Neil heard him repeating what they had said, and then someone else suggested, "So someone had better go and look for her there, then."

The muttering became more hostile. Neil

heard someone mention the police, but a louder voice called out, "No, we'll see to it ourselves! They're on our land."

A chorus agreed with him. "Let's go up there now!" another voice shouted. "We'll find young Penny and turn those dirty travellers out!"

Kate and Glen exchanged an alarmed glance. The sound of the meeting had suddenly become very ugly. "Let's get out of here," Kate said. "Your parents will kill us if we let you get mixed up in a riot."

She put an arm on Julie's shoulder to propel her towards the street leading out of the square, and everyone else followed.

"Shouldn't we tell someone?" Emily said. "It's our fault it's happening – because they heard what I said."

"The police could stop it," Julie suggested.

"We ought to warn Keziah and the gypsies," said Neil.

"You're right," said Glen, coming to a halt on the street corner. "Listen. The rest of you go with Kate and the dogs. Warn the gypsies but stay out of trouble yourselves. I'll find the police station, tell them what's happening, and join you as soon as I can."

He darted away, around the edge of the

square, avoiding the knot of people that was growing larger and noisier by the minute.

Kate led Neil and the others at a brisk pace down the street and the noise gradually died away behind them.

"Maybe they'll see sense," Kate said, "or maybe the police will stop them before they get very far. But we're not going to take any chances."

The sun was starting to go down as they hurried along the road. Just before they reached the turning to Ainsworth Castle a car passed them, driven by Adrian Bartlett, with Lord Ainsworth in the passenger seat. Neil signalled frantically, but neither of the men saw him.

"What did you want with them?" Emily asked.

"I wanted to tell them what's going on. Lord Ainsworth might be able to stop the villagers."

"I'll go after them, if you like," Max offered. "It's not far."

Kate hesitated and then said, "All right. But once you're there, stay there. I don't want you wandering around on your own. This could be dangerous. You're not in *The Time Travellers* now."

Max grinned and jogged off down the road to the castle with Prince at his heels.

"See Prince has a rest!" Neil yelled after him.

He was worrying that the villagers might pass them in their cars and get to the gypsy camp before they could give the warning. But no one had appeared by the time they reached the lane.

Once they were off the road, Neil and Emily quickened their pace until they were running, with Kate and Julie at their heels and Sam bounding alongside.

In the gypsy camp, everything was quiet. A few of the gypsies were sitting round the fire, and Keziah was seated on the steps of her *vardo*, with Chavi at her feet. She was mending a skirt, and listening to the news on a portable radio.

Emily dashed towards her. "It's the villagers! They're coming! They think you've got Penny!"

Chapter Ten

"*Sarishan*, Emily," said Keziah. Her needle flashed as she set in the last couple of stitches and folded her sewing away. She switched off the radio. "Sit down. Tell me properly."

Emily flopped down, panting, beside Chavi. Julie sat on the dog's other side, and stroked her ears. "Didn't you know about this, Chavi?"

"Penny Ainsworth from the castle has gone missing," Neil explained, squatting on the lowest step of the *vardo*. "And her dog. Her father can't find them anywhere."

"The villagers think she's come here," Emily said, still catching her breath.

"Or – or that you stole her," Julie added.

Keziah's face hardened. "These are the tales they tell about the Rom," she said. "But there is no truth in it. They may come and search, if they will."

"I'm sorry, Keziah." Kate brushed away wisps of hair that clung to her face after the effort of running. "They sounded violent. They might – well, they might do more than just search."

Keziah gave her a long look.

"Glen went to the police," Kate added. "But they might not come in time."

Very slowly and deliberately, Keziah got to her feet. She smoothed her skirts, and looked around the camp. "Nat! Tibo! Joseph!"

The gypsies, with Rick among them, came to stand around in a half-circle. Keziah gestured to Neil. "Tell them."

Neil repeated the story of what was happening in Beckthwaite. "Hurry!" he finished. "You've got to do something. They'll be here any minute."

Now the gypsies were muttering among themselves; Neil thought they looked just as dangerous as the villagers. With a cold feeling in his stomach he thought, *There's going to be a fight.*

"Have any of you seen this girl in our camp?" Keziah asked. "Rick, have you?"

The way she spoke to Rick made Neil realize that Keziah too knew something about Rick and Penny.

Rick just shook his head. "No, Keziah. I haven't seen her since yesterday. I'd have told you if I had."

Keziah nodded. Nat shouted, "They'll never believe us. We're Rom. They think we're all liars and thieves."

"That may be so," Keziah said. "But we will tell them the truth, and we will let them search our camp. There will be no fighting unless the *gaujos* strike first."

There was still some muttering, but Neil could see the gypsies would accept what Keziah told them.

Before anyone could move, the sound of a car engine cut through the quiet, and an old blue van came jolting down the lane and pulled up at the edge of the clearing. Half a dozen men from the village climbed out and walked menacingly across to the group of gypsies. A couple of them were carrying stout sticks; one had a shotgun.

Keziah came down the steps of the *vardo* and confronted them. "*Sarishan*, friends," she said calmly. "What is it you want?"

The man with the shotgun stepped forward. "You've got young Penny Ainsworth here. We want her back."

"She is not here," said Keziah.

"That's what you say!" one of the other men shouted, shouldering his way forward. "Do you think we'll believe a dirty gypsy?"

Nat started furiously towards him, but one look from Keziah made him step back.

"You may search," Keziah said. She stood back and gestured towards her own door. "Start here, with my *vardo*."

Kate grabbed Neil's shoulder, and pushed

Emily and Julie away from the crowd and towards the lakeshore path. "Come on. There's nothing we can do."

"But Kate—" Emily protested.

"No buts. What would your mum say if—" Kate broke off as Neil suddenly tore free and dashed off through the undergrowth. "Neil! Come back here!"

"Wait a minute!" Neil called back, not sure whether Kate had heard. He had been looking round for Rick; once the villagers arrived he had vanished. Neil wondered whether he was mixed up somehow with Penny's disappearance, or whether he was trying to avoid a fight.

Just as Kate was herding everyone down the path, Neil had caught a glimpse of Chavi, slipping ghostlike through the camp. He dashed across to intercept her, but stopped sharply as the Weimaraner sniffed out a dark figure hiding behind a tree. He heard Rick's voice.

"Chavi? No, Chavi, I can't."

The Weimaraner had hold of Rick's shirtsleeve again, and began pulling him gently along the path towards Ainsworth Castle. Rick stopped resisting, and went with her.

Neil heard him say, "What is it, girl? Do

you know where Penny is?"

He followed Rick and the dog, without trying to catch up, but keeping them in sight as the path meandered through the bushes. Sam pattered along behind him, and after a minute Kate overtook him with Emily and Julie.

"Neil, what are you playing at?" she asked, exasperated.

"It's Chavi," Neil explained. "She's taking Rick to the castle. She knows something! We've got to follow them!"

Kate shrugged. "OK. So long as we stay out of trouble."

From the camp behind them came the sounds of angry voices, crashing and the neighing of horses as the villagers made their search, but the noise died away as they drew closer to the castle. Emily kept glancing over her shoulder. "I hate leaving Keziah."

"Glen's fetching the police," Kate reminded her. "And maybe Max can get Lord Ainsworth to help."

"Look!" said Neil suddenly. "What's Rick doing now?"

He was close enough to hear Rick exclaim, "Chavi – yes, I see! Good girl!" He started to run.

112

Neil and the rest had to run to keep up with him. Sam began barking excitedly.

When they came to the castle Rick dashed straight across the causeway, underneath the arch, and up the steps to the huge iron-studded doors. Chavi bounded beside him. As Neil and the others came panting into the courtyard, Rick began banging on the doors and shouting, "Open up! Let me in!"

The doors swung wide and Rick shot inside, almost knocking Adrian Bartlett off his feet. Crowding up behind, Neil saw the steward was looking white and shocked.

Adrian Bartlett said nothing but followed Rick as he ran across the stone-flagged hallway and through a pair of inner doors. Then he turned back and gave Neil a bewildered look. "What is this?"

"I don't know," said Neil. "But it's OK. I think Rick knows where Penny is."

Another man, who had been standing at the side of the hall, moved forward. "I seem to have come at a bad time . . ."

Neil recognized Brian Mason, the director of *The Time Travellers*, and remembered Adrian Bartlett had said he was coming to look at the castle.

Mr Bartlett tossed a few words of apology over his shoulder as he followed Rick. Neil pressed up behind him, and found himself in an enormous pillared hall. The floor was paved with stone. The warm light of sunset poured in through high windows with pointed arches. Tattered banners hung from the rafters.

At the far end of the hall was a huge fireplace, surrounded by stone carvings. Chavi waited alertly beside it. There wasn't a fire, and the space was big enough for Rick to step right inside it. He twisted one of the carvings, and Neil caught his breath as he saw part of the stone swing back.

Rick called out sharply, "Penny! Come out of there, right now!"

Penny's voice said, "Richie? Is that really you?"

"Yes it is. Now will you please come out?" He sounded impatient.

There was a bark, and King appeared out of the gap between the stones and hurled himself at Rick just as he had done the day before in the woods. As Rick staggered under the impact, Penny emerged from the gap; King rushed towards her and then back to Rick, as if he couldn't decide which of them he wanted to be

with most. Neil couldn't believe he was seeing
the huge, dignified dog go so crazy with
delight.

"Penny!" Rick sounded furious. "What are
you playing at? The whole village has been
looking for you? They're tearing the gypsy camp
apart, and—"

Penny wailed, "Richie!" and threw her arms
round him. Rick stopped what he had been
saying and hugged her tightly.

Neil said, "Will somebody tell me what's going
on?"

"It's a secret passage!" Emily exclaimed.

"She was there all the time," Julie added.

"A priest's hole, actually," Mr Bartlett said. He was beaming delightedly. "In all my years here I didn't even know Ainsworth Castle had one!"

Rick and Penny were still hugging. Kate started to say, "I'm really sorry for barging in like this—" Brian Mason spoke at the same time. "Mr Bartlett, this is a splendid room. I could just see the round table here."

Before Mr Bartlett could reply to either of them, there was the sound of more people entering the hall. Neil turned to see Lord Ainsworth and Glen with Max and Prince, with Keziah close behind. Emily flew across to her. "Keziah! Is everything all right?"

Neil didn't hear what Keziah said in reply. His eyes were riveted on Rick. The violinist released Penny as Lord Ainsworth stopped dead, staring.

"Richard!" he exclaimed.

Still with an arm round Penny's shoulders, Rick took a couple of steps back down the hall and said, "Hello, Dad."

"You mean that Rick is your *brother*?" said Neil.

Penny laughed; Neil had never seen her

looking really happy before. "Yes. He ran away a year ago because our dad wouldn't let him study music."

"So *that's* how he plays so well."

"Yes. He got a place at music college, but Daddy said he had to stay at home and learn how to manage the estate. Rick swore that if he couldn't do what he wanted he would go away and never set foot on Ainsworth land again. So when I saw him yesterday I knew I had to think of some way to make him come back."

Everyone was sitting in what Lord Ainsworth called the Small Drawing Room. Neil reckoned you could have fitted all the ground floor of their house at King Street Kennels into it.

Sam, Prince, Chavi and King were sprawled together on the hearthrug. King's head was raised, as if he was proud to welcome them into his home. The human guests were making themselves comfortable on shabby chairs and sofas. Lord Ainsworth had insisted on opening a bottle of wine to celebrate Rick's homecoming, and Penny had brought fruit juice for Neil and the others.

"So you shut yourself and King up in the priest's hole," Lord Ainsworth said to her.

"That was extremely stupid."

"And it wasn't good for King," said Rick.

"I know." Penny was too happy to look really sorry. "If you hadn't come today, I would have sneaked out with him tonight to feed him and give him a run."

"And how did you know Rick would find you? Emily asked.

"Rick used to play hide-and-seek with me in the priest's hole when I was little," Penny explained. "It was our special place."

"To be honest," said Rick, "I'd forgotten about it at first. Then Chavi brought me here, and I put two and two together." He reached a hand down to Chavi, who was lying at his feet, and caressed her silky ears. "You're a great dog, Chavi."

He gave Keziah an embarrassed smile. Rather to Neil's surprise, the gypsy woman was sitting at her ease beside Lord Ainsworth with a glass of wine in her hand.

"You'll be leaving us now, *Boshengro*," she said. It wasn't a question. "This is your place."

"I'm sorry for going off like that, but I haven't changed my mind," Rick said, frowning stubbornly. Neil suddenly realized who Rick

reminded him of. He looked exactly like his father! "Dad, I've got to study music. It's what I'm good at."

"And what about Ainsworth Castle?" his father snapped back at him. "Your place is here. This . . . er . . . lady" – he waved a hand at Keziah – "just said so. Ainsworth Castle needs an heir."

"Is there any reason I can't do both?" Rick asked.

"That's all very well, but where's the money coming from?"

"I think I might help with that, sir." It was Brian Mason who spoke; he and Adrian Bartlett had been sitting at one side with their heads together. "This castle is perfect for Camelot in the *Time Travellers* feature film. If you'll allow us to film here, of course the company will pay you."

"And we'll attract more visitors," Mr Bartlett said. "They'll come to see the place where the film was made."

"You could offer all kinds of attractions," Brian suggested. "Displays of costumes, photographs . . . Other places have done it."

"The stars could come and sign autographs," Max added.

"Now just a minute," said Lord Ainsworth. "I haven't agreed to any of this. Remember this is Ainsworth Castle we're talking about, not some shoddy theme park."

"Oh, Daddy!" Penny wailed.

Adrian Bartlett's eyes danced with amusement, though he was straight-faced as he said, "There are other ways, of course, sir. We could run a funfair. Karaoke nights. Fifty pence to shake hands with a real live lord . . ."

"Adrian!" Lord Ainsworth exploded. "Have you taken leave of your senses?"

Rick laughed. "Adrian will talk him round. The film's a perfect solution. There'll be money for repairs, and for my music course—"

"And King's operation," Neil interrupted.

"Yes, of course," Rick said. "That's first on the list. Thank goodness you spotted it, Neil."

He bent over King and examined his eyes carefully. King gazed back at him and Neil could see the great dog felt a deep satisfaction at being reunited with his friend.

"So King will be fine," said Emily. "And the castle won't fall down, because there'll be enough money to run it, and – and Lord Ainsworth will have an heir again!"

"Now I get it," said Neil. "That's what you and your dad were so worried about, Penny. Rick had disappeared."

"It was awful," said Penny. "Nobody knew where he was. We never thought he'd run away with the gypsies!"

"I've a lot to thank them for," Rick said seriously. "I met them last time they stayed beside the lake. They knew I had a musician's heart in me straight away. Keziah," he added, turning to the gypsy woman, "I'm sorry, I forgot to ask – is everything all right in the camp?"

"Of course, or I would not be here," Keziah replied. "The police and Lord Ainsworth arrived at the same time, and the villagers suddenly remembered they had important things to see to at home." She smiled and bowed her head to Lord Ainsworth. "The Rom do not often come under a *gaujo*'s roof. But I felt I must thank you, Lord Ainsworth, and make sure this foolish boy had come to no harm."

"Foolish boy!" Rick exclaimed, going scarlet.

"We're agreed on that, at least, ma'am," Lord Ainsworth said grimly. He got to his feet and raised his glass of wine. Looking embarrassed, he added, "And perhaps we can drink to friendship. If you and your people come here again, ma'am, you'll be welcome to camp on Ainsworth land. And so will you," he added to Kate and Glen. "I can see I owe you an apology."

"Several, actually," Neil murmured, but not so that anyone could hear.

Keziah rose, too, and clinked glasses with Lord Ainsworth. "*Kushto bokht,* lord. Emily, can you tell him what that means?"

"It's Romany for 'good luck'," Emily said.

"I'll drink to that, ma'am."

"*Kushto bokht,*" Rick echoed, and King barked a deep-toned agreement.

Everyone raised their glasses. Neil looked around the circle of smiling faces. Even King, he thought, seemed to be smiling, and as for Chavi, her jaws were gaping in a wide grin. Nobody could possibly doubt that good luck had returned to Ainsworth Castle at last.

PUPPY PATROL titles available from Macmillan Children's Books

The prices shown below are correct at the time of going to press. However, Macmillan Publishers reserve the right to show new retail prices on covers which may differ from those previously advertised.

JENNY DALE

1.	Teacher's Pet	0 330 34905 8	£2.99
2.	Big Ben	0 330 34906 6	£2.99
3.	Abandoned!	0 330 34907 4	£2.99
4.	Double Trouble	0 330 34908 2	£2.99
5.	Star Paws	0 330 34909 0	£2.99
6.	Tug of Love	0 330 34910 4	£2.99
7.	Saving Skye	0 330 35492 2	£2.99
8.	Tuff's Luck	0 330 35493 0	£2.99
9.	Red Alert	0 330 36937 7	£2.99
10.	The Great Escape	0 330 36938 5	£2.99
11.	Perfect Puppy	0 330 36939 3	£2.99
12.	Sam & Delilah	0 330 36940 7	£2.99
13.	The Sea Dog	0 330 37039 1	£2.99
14.	Puppy School	0 330 37040 5	£2.99
15.	A Winter's Tale	0 330 37041 3	£2.99
16.	Puppy Love	0 330 37042 1	£2.99
17.	Best of Friends	0 330 37043 X	£2.99
18.	King of the Castle	0 330 37392 7	£2.99
19.	Posh Pup	0 330 37393 5	£2.99
20.	Charlie's Choice	0 330 37394 3	£2.99

All Macmillan titles can be ordered at your local bookshop or are available by post from:

Book Service by Post
PO Box 29, Douglas, Isle of Man IM99 1BQ

Credit cards accepted. For details:
Telephone: 01624 675137
Fax: 01624 670923
E-mail: bookshop@enterprise.net

Free postage and packing in the UK.
Overseas customers: add £1 per book (paperback)
and £3 per book (hardback).